"If You Do Not Know My Story,

You Won't Understand My Praise."

By: Shaniqua L. Jackson

Introductions

Many people are misjudged by the way they look, carry themselves, or even the way they speak. You never know what the next person is going through, unless you are like a psychic or something, but even then, they do not know everything. I would like to take the time out to say, never judge a book by its cover, because you will possibly miss out on getting to know an amazing person on the inside. I remember one day, I saw this guy dressed up in all black with chains and all types of body piercings, and I went to ask him, "sir, why do you have on all black and do all those piercings hurt," "he then said, "No, they don't hurt but I wear all black because it represents Gotham, and I'm expressing my inner self." I then sat there and asked him to explain that to me and after doing so I found it was so interesting. I told him I was going to try it out and see if I can see what my inner self tells me or where it may lead me. The next day I went to school in all black, I could not get those piercings because my parents would have flipped out. Upon going to school the next day, everyone looked at me like I was crazy as I walked in with my black outfit on. It was as if I had risen from the dead, or some sort. They were so afraid of me and called me a freak and many other names, but instead of taking the time out to get to know me they judged me because I was different. I found this confusing because unlike me, they were not curious about the change in my appearance as I was about, that young man, I had met the day before. Yet they judged me and criticized me for the changes I had made without question. I say that to say this, "never take anyone or anything for granted, because you never know when you may hurt someone or miss out on making a new friend. Life is too short to take lightly, so live every moment like it is your last.

Acknowledgements

First, I want to give honor to God who is the head of my life and for allowing me to be able to write this book and my church family, and many more. I would also like to take the time to thank my biggest supporter "Darrien Higgs", without him a lot of my inspiration to write songs or write poetry, would never be published, or heard of. I also would like to thank my mom Lila and Dad Gent; may he rest in peace, for raising me to be the great mother I am today. I would also like to give a special thanks to the woman the keeps our family together, "The One and Only, Willene Wright", this woman is my biggest fan, and I love her so much. Grandma, thank you for being so strong, loving, giving, and well respected. You are truly a woman of God and it is my great pleasure to be your granddaughter. May God continue to bless you and keep you covered with his grace and mercy. I love you I admire your strength and wanted to have your strength as my own. For your acknowledgment, thanks for taking the time out to help me understand myself for who I am, I say thank you. I know God is doing amazing things with you and because of you, I am finding more of me, thank you Momma Mary. And for anyone I missed do not think I forgot about you. I love my whole family and all of you for being in my life graciously.

Content

Chapters

1. **The Beginning**

In the beginning there was a little girl born in Bronx, NY to a single mother who already had two other children. The little's girl name was Lanai Tiana Jenkins, and her mother name was Diane Jenkins. Lanai sister was a year older than her and her brother was two years older than her. Their names were Brianna and Jason. Lanai was born on August 10, 1984 @ 3 a.m..When Lanai left the hospital with her mother Diane, she was the most adorable brown skin, bright eyed little baby. Lanai siblings were already separated from her mother Diane by the time she was born because, her mother Diane was young when she had them, and she was not ready to be responsible to raise them. Lanai was two weeks old when her mother brought her home, where she lived with her sister Porsha. Porsha was in the living room watching a movie and heard her niece Lanai crying so loud from Diane's room and was wondering why her mother Diane was not tending to her. Porsha got so frustrated and started walking towards Diane's room, upon opening the door she found Diane on the bed sleep. Diane jumped up realizing her baby was not laying next to her.

Diane jumped up panicking, “where is she”? She then followed the baby scream on the side of the bed, between the bed and the wall. Push the bed from the wall and reached down from the tangled sheets and grabbed Lanai to her chest and started crying hysterically at that point, Porsha realized that Diane was not ready yet again to take care another child. Porsha closed the door leaving Diane sitting on the bed holding Lanai to then called her Brother John and Sister-in-law Betty to come and get Lanai and raise her. Lanai aunt and uncle had one son of their own named Sean. He was about seven years older than Lanai. The couple came from Washington, DC to pick up Lanai. Upon arriving two hours later to Porsha’s house, Diane opened the door, puzzled to see her brother John and his wife Betty. Diane said to her brother “Let me guess, Porsha Called you didn’t she”? Diane let her brother in and then yelled for Porsha to come in the living room. Diane, John, Porsha, & Betty all sat in the living drinking tea coming up with a game plan for Lanai. Diane said to John I really do not want to let my baby go, but I know I can not provide for her like you can. Diane accepted this and asked that they take good care of her baby. She closed the door with tears in her eyes. As John and Betty leaves to return home Lanai was crying and they did not understand what was wrong with her. Betty got in the back seat with Lanai and held her in her arms, rocked her until she fell asleep. Years went by and now Lanai is five years old and was a mascot for her brother/cousin football team. Although she really knew something was different about the two of them, Lanai waited to question the situation. At the time of Lanai departure from her mom, she was too young to understand that people who entered her life where not whom they appeared to be. As time went by, Lanai knew she was different from her then known as brother Sean. She became curious one day and asked her mom why she was funny looking from Sean. Betty knew she would have to have this conversation with the child, but was not expecting to do so at the age of five. When Betty had gotten through explaining Lanai's life events to her, she could tell the child was sad. She went to the fridge and had gotten an ice cream sandwich and told Lanai to come here. Baby girl, life is never what we grown folks would like for it to be, but one thing is for sure with us we love you and would do anything for you. Do you understand what I am saying? She said, handing the ice cream sandwich to Lanai. Yes mam. I understand. So, my mom was sick and could not take care of me? That is right sug, she was sick. But that does not mean she did not love you. She loved you so much that she asked me and your uncle to take care of you for her. She will always be a part of your life. Ok then, so do I have to stop calling you momma? No, baby, you keep on doing that. Betty said hugging her. Now Lanai, seemed very happy at this point, she found out the truth about herself and why she looked so funny from Sean and she got some ice cream to seal the hurt. Lanai is now nine years old and had to move to South Carolina with the family. Lanai did not want to move but she was too young to make any decisions. Lanai was upset that she had to leave all her friends and start over but then she started a new school and tried to fit in. Lanai always had a friendly spirit about her and always was so easily influence. She was in a new area and felt intimidated by the kids because they were so mean. Lanai tried every day to make friends and it seem like it got harder and harder, until one day a girl name Diamond came up to her and said, “I’ll be your friend”, and ever since then they were inseparable.

Diamond knew the ropes to the school, and pretty much knew everyone. She broke it down to Lanai on who she can and can not talk to and trust in school. Every day after school, Lanai would tell her mom/aunt Betty how she did not like the school here, nor the kids, because they would pick on her and call her all types of names. Even though she met one great person, she still felt like an outsider. Lanai then started having a crush on this boy in school. He was more on the popular side and his name was David. One day, Lanai was running outside at the playground and was not looking where she was going, she then bumped into David and fell on the ground. Although David was popular, he was different from the rest. He helped Lanai off the ground while his friends laughed and asked her, "are you alright?", Lanai smiled at him and said, "yes, thanks." The next day, David asked, "would you like to hangout sometimes. Lanai said, "of

Course, excitedly"! Time goes by and now Lanai is in middle school seventh-eighth grade. Her friends have now expanded to more people getting to know her for who she really was. Even though Diamond and David were still her friends she became friends with a girl named Desiree. Desiree lived around corner from her with her father named Dan. Desiree had lost her mother at a young age, so her father raised her. Lanai and Desiree would do everything together, from walking to school too writing poetry to see who could write the most. Desiree always wrote more than Lanai. Middle School life was much easier for Lanai but there were a few who treated her like she was a nobody. By the time middle school was over her friend David had to move to Scranton, SC where he finished off his school. So, at that time David never knew Lanai true feelings about him. Lanai friend Diamond and Desiree held down the friendship clan, until more friends came into the picture. At this point they were beginning high school. Even though Lanai had friends at Manning High School, which was her school, she also had friends at her rivalry school Scott Branch. Scott Branch was a school that her cousins attended, and she wanted to go there so bad, but her mom/aunt Betty did not want her to go there because she did not live in the area. Lanai tried out for the cheerleading squad, but the girls did not like her, so she did not make the team. That never stopped her, she was in JROTC, she was on the band, and she was even on the step team. Lanai crew she hung with between Manning High and Scott Branch were girls that were on another level than her. They were more experienced with boys and Lanai was never with a boy. While they were together, Lanai would sit back and listen to their conversations about who did what with who and she did not have no news to talk about. Then she started making up stories about different boys, so she would fit in and will not feel left out. When Lanai started her sophomore year in high school, she was so in love with this football player named Darnell, or at least she thought she was in love. He never talked with her like that until afterschool when no one was around and when he would call her on the phone. Darnell had graduate two years before Lanai and he went into the Navy. Even though Darnell was in the Navy he stayed in touch with Lanai by phone. There was this other guy who was Lanai friend in school, he was a little different from most because he wore all black and worship Gotham type stuff. Even though he was weird, she still liked him, and they dated for a while on the low because they parents worked together at Burger King. This guy name was (Daniel) and he also graduated two years before Lanai. They lost contact for a while because he was a trouble guy and always got sick from a blood disorder. Lanai never could handle him being sick, because she was afraid of losing him and she just wanted to stay friends. Even though they were meant for one another she did not know how to accept his sickness at the time.

Best Friend

Lanai group of best friends were Daniel, Diamond, Desiree, and David. These were the people that Lanai trusted the most at the time of growing up in high school. Daniel was my best friend and my first true love, because he knew the meaning of love before I did, and he taught me how to love. Even though we lost contact, we always found a way to stay in touch, even if it was through his mom or sister. His sister (Maryann) was always like a sister to me. She was younger but always was loyal. His mom was like a mom to me, her name was Teresa. They always kept me informed when Daniel was sick or in the hospital. There had been times I was able to go visit but not all the time. While in high school, Lanai first date was to the military ball and Daniel escorted her there, and he did not wear black either. He dressed up real nice. Lanai was so nervous, after that night he kissed her and that was her first kiss ever. That was when Lanai knew she had really liked him but did not want to ruin a friendship. Diamond was her next true friend and always was a ride or die type person. Lanai and Diamond would walk around school with a ruler and their favorite line to joke on people was, "Damn big shoe, let me measure them boats you wearing". Lanai and Diamond was a force to reckon with together they did not know how to act. Today those two are still best of friends and still at it with the ruler joke. Diamond would always laugh so hard and loud every time she is around Lanai. Lanai loved the fact that Diamond was always the same and never changed for no one. Diamond would always joke with Lanai and say, "hey big shoe, u bend over and bust it open lately." Lanai, would laugh so hard and say, "Girl you know I did, and you know this man!!!" Them, two did not know what to say out of their mouth sometimes. Desiree became a distant friend once she transferred from Manning High School to go to Scott branch. She completed the rest of her high school years there. Even though we were in different schools she still was there for me, because when I got pregnant my junior year going into my senior year with my daughter, she was there the whole time. Desiree even threw Lanai first baby shower also named Lanai's daughter. Lanai daughter name is La'Shay and she was born on Sept 20, 2002. Once she was born Desiree spoiled her so much and took her to take her first pictures. We did many things together and I gave her the privilege of being La'shay's godmother. I remember our Junior Year in high school I was invited to Desiree's prom by this guy named Lenall, and when I got there he was not there yet. Desiree saw me at the door, and I told her I was waiting on my date Lenall to show up and she said, "girl come in as my guest, until he gets here". I said, "thanks girl, I appreciate it." Lanai did not like the fact of just standing there alone, anyway. Once Desiree and Lanai entered the prom they went to the table and drunk some punch and talked about what everyone had planned after that night. Around ten o'clock Lenall decided to finally show up to the prom and Desiree introduced Lanai to him. "Lenall, Desiree said, "this is Lanai". Lenall just looked at her and said, "hi, how are you," and Lanai said, "I'm fine and yourself." Basically, after they spoke Lenall went and completely ignored the fact Lanai existed. Even though Lanai thought that night was going to be different, she did not let that ruin her night of having fun. Desiree and Lanai begin dancing and mingling with everyone else. By midnight when the prom was over Lanai went home instead of hanging out with everyone because she had a child to go home too. David was her last friend that Lanai consider her best friend. David was not around a lot until later in Lanai life. Lanai and David reunited once Lanai had already had her second child which you will hear more about later in the story. Lanai best friend list did not end there. She had friend at Scott Branch, she has not discussed. Their names are Melody, Shaunta, China, and many others that she admires, but these three were her ace crew. Melody is her main friend, her ace of all trades, her ride or die who will always have her back no matter what happens. They met while they were on the stepp team and still today are close as ever. Shaunta and China became distance after high school which was understandable because they all went on different career and journey. Even though Shaunta and China had drifted from the crew, they still made contact by social media to say hi to one another. Lanai and Desiree connected again at college, where lanai learned that Desiree had been mischievous by slandering her name about her kids and kids' father. Lanai had come back home from Texas, where she was living with her daughter Patience father who had put them out. Desiree had rumors so bad about Lanai she was very upset. Lanai then strayed away from being friends with Desiree. As time went by Desiree and Lanai was never close again. Friends come a dime a dozen, do not take them for granted.

Betrayal

Is Betrayal supposed to hurt? Is Betrayal supposed to make you cry? Lanai knew betrayal all so well because so many people have betrayed her in so many ways. Kevin invited Lanai to Texas to rekindle their love and to see if they were really meant to be. Lanai was only twenty years old and felt like moving to Texas was a way to get away from her uncle/dad John. After six months of living with Kevin, Lanai felt she was being smothered. Kevin was controlling, disrespectful, and everything had to be his way or the highway. On Lanai's birthday she wanted to call home, but Kevin said to Lanai "stop acting like a child"! Later that night Kevin allowed Lanai to call her mother to only find her uncle/father John was sick and not doing to well. Lanai was very sad and was ready to return home. Kevin then stated, "get dress we're going out to celebrate with my brother Mark and his wife Kelly." Lanai, Mark, Kevin, & Kelly all arrived at Club Exclusive. Lanai & Kevin dance the night away and took her mind off things back home with her uncle/father John. When Lanai and Kevin returned home, Kevin started being aggressive because he wanted to be intimate with Lanai and she was just to tired. Kevin did not care that Lanai was tired, he took advantage of her. The next morning Lanai went to use the payphone down the road to call her grandmother Pearl and asked her "what is Uncle Charles number? Uncle Charles lived two hours away from Lanai in Dallas Texas. Lanai called her uncle and advised him where she was and asked if he would come get her and the kids for the weekend. By the time Lanai got back to the house Kevin brother Mark had called him and said, “bro I think Lanai is leaving” she at the house packing the kids up and she called someone to get her. Kevin got home early and began questioning Lanai like she was one of his kids. Lanai said to Kevin, honestly, I do not have to answer to you. Lanai walked away from Kevin and started putting her stuff by the door and Kevin stated, “you can go and visit your family, but my child isn’t going.” Lanai then stated, “YOU GOT ME FUCKED UP,” SHE IS GOING WHEREVER I GO! Kevin picked Patience up and held on to her the whole entire time. What Lanai did not know at the time is that if one parent has the child in their arms law enforcement can not force that parent to release the child to the other parent. Lanai called Kevin’s mother and told her everything that was going on hoping she would convince her son to give Lanai her child back and Kevin would not listen to his mother either. Local Law enforcement units came, and Lanai Uncle Charles showed up at the same time. The police officer advised Lanai that she will have to return to South Carolina and obtain a lawyer to get her daughter Patience back. Lanai cried and pleaded with Kevin to give Patience to her and he stated no over and over again. Patience got in the car with her uncle Charles and they proceeded to head to his home in Dallas. Charles paid for Lanai and her two years old daughter La'Shay a bus ticket back home. Betrayal for Lanai had just begun in Texas with Patience father. When Lanai got back home her first thing to do was to get her a lawyer. Lanai did not have the money to pay for a lawyer so her grandmother Pearl loaned her the money until she could get on her feet. Patience was only nine months when Lanai had to leave her child with Kevin. Lanai returned to South Carolina From Texas she decided to go back to school. She went to Morris College where she knew a few of her friends attended thinking that would be a good thing, but come to find out that's when a lot of drama began. Desiree was supposed to be Lanai ace boon coon, ride or die friend, but Lanai always felt she was jealous of her. Desiree would spread rumors about Lanai on campus and she was so disappointed in her so-called friend. Once Lanai learned the truth, she then left school and just decided to go on another path. While on that other path she then reconnected with her long-lost friend David. David was the guy that she ran into in third grade and their family was always close because his aunt Lenora always included Lanai in their family functions. Even though they were ok with Lanai and David friendship, they never wanted him to get involved with Lanai on a serious level. For some reason they felt Lanai was not worthy of him and she would lead him down the wrong path from the rumors about Lanai in that small town. People never really knew Lanai just what they heard about her and who she was around. David and Lanai then, started dating slowly behind their family back, but David was living in Aiken and Lanai lived in Manning. Lanai convinced David to come move with her and work at the warehouse where her brother was a supervisor so they could be together. They were a power couple once he moved here and even though his family did not approve of them being together, that was not going to stop them from being great together. They then moved out of Lanai's mom house into their own place down the road from Lanai's mom, and Lanai was pregnant with their child. When David came into Lanai life, she had already had two kids and that is why his family did not want him getting involved with her. At that point, her children were two and four years old. David was all they knew as a father figure. Once they moved in their place, Lanai was working as a dispatcher for Clarendon County while carrying her son and David had worked for Food lion Warehouse. David would have a drink here and there when they would go out to her brother/cousin Sean's house or have gatherings at their home, but it was not as bad. When their son was born David was already out of work from an accident he had and never went back to the warehouse. He then begins working at sears and would slack off with helping with bills and started drinking more and living the single life like Lanai did not exist. She would always tell David until you get on your feet, she will hold it down. David had lost his job from sears and had to be at home with the kids and for some reason, Lanai did not let him down still had his back and took care of home. David realized it was a lot on Lanai to handle so David started grinding by doing side jobs with his uncle Shawn. Even though David had that side job, it did not stop David from drinking all the time and hanging out. David and Lanai son was born on December 21, 2009 and they named him David Jr. Lanai thought things would have changed with David's attitude once their son was born but it did not. David started cheating and

Lanai got so fed up with having to do everything, she reached out to his auntie Lenora and asked if they could move in with her so she could help with the children and it would be less stress on Lanai. Lenora always was like family to Lanai regardless how anyone else in their family felt about Lanai. Lanai then lost her job with the sheriff department after being there a year. Lanai was sent to the academy twice to get state certified, but because Lanai had so much going on in her personal life, she could not focus on the academy to pass the test. Lanai then begin working little side end jobs to make ends meet and while she was on her grind and being a provider David still did his own thing. Lanai was always a go getter and never really was the type to stop striving for excellence. Lanai was offered a job in Atlanta, GA as a nonemergency dispatcher for a transport company. When Lanai first went to the job, she did not have a place to stay so she ended up staying with a girl she met through a family member. Lanai left her kids with Lenora while she went there to get situated and on her feet. After being there a month, Lanai got snowed in and had to catch rides to work and David decided he wanted to come visit. Even after explaining to David she did not have a place for him to stay up there he still came and messed a lot up for Lanai. For some odd reason David thought Lanai was cheating on him with his cousin Craig that lived in Atlanta. Lanai met his cousin once at wedding and saw Craig again when she was in the mall, he asked her to try his detox product. Craig had told Lanai about a police officer position with the sheriff department in Atlanta and Lanai applied but never got the position. David had left Atlanta after three days of being there to go back home. Lanai had met with a family a week later to look at a house to try and move David and the kids there, but she received a call from David stating that his grandmother was in critical condition and she wasn't going to make it. Lanai then quit her job and went back home to help with the family issues. When Lanai was moving forward something always set her back. Once his grandmother passed it really took a toll on David. Lanai and David had been together for 6 years and was engaged and still having problems. Lanai and David went to her brother/cousin Sean's house one night for a card game and they were racking up on winning a lot of money. David started drinking extremely to much, so Lanai said, "David lets go home its late," David stated no I am good.

Now its like three thirty in the morning and Lanai put the kids in the vehicle and drove to Lenora house where they lived. When they got in the driveway Lanai put the car in park and David then said, "did you sleep with my cousin Craig, and Lanai said, "NO, what is wrong with you and what possessed you to ask me that? David then reached over to the driver side and choked Lanai so hard and she was starting to lose consciousness, when her daughter La'Shay woke up out of her sleep in the back and said, "DON'T KILL MY MOMMY!" Lanai got out of the vehicle and ran in the house to go get a knife and yelled out to Lenora to get her nephew David before she killed him. His mother Laura came in the living room and grabbed him, and Lanai grabbed their son out the bed and said to David do not you ever put your hands on me again.

Laura and Lenora were trying to figure out why he put his hand on Lanai and she explained it to them once she calmed down. David was constantly begging Lanai not to call her brother/cousin Sean and he would have rather her call the police. Instead Lanai packed her things and left and moved back in with her mother. Lanai and David went their separate ways and even though their relationship went south Lanai kept in touch with David and his family. They were friends so long and even though he hurt her, Lanai still wanted him to stay active in their child life. Lanai started working with the Orangeburg County Sheriff department as a Telecommunication Specialist. While working there she Dated this Guy that worked on the force named Eli. When Lanai first met Eli, she did not even know who he was. Everyone always use to say to

Lanai, how u and Eli doing and Lanai would always respond, "who is this man ya'll claiming I go with?" One day Eli had to come by dispatch for some paperwork and Lanai said, "so you're the infamous Eli I'm suppose to be dating, and Eli was confused but he had the same response." They exchanged numbers and made their relationship into a reality. They would hangout at his apartment and did other things if you know what I mean, and everything was amazing. Then one day Eli disappeared off the face of the earth and Lanai never heard from him again. Lanai was heartbroken and just did not understand what happen and where did they go wrong. Lanai felt love was just not for her and started feeling depressed. Lanai had to figure out some things in her life and understand what was missing. In the mist of finding herself she had to go get a copy of her birth certificate for her job one day and notice a name she did not recognized a name on there and asked to have it removed. When lanai got home, she did some research on Facebook with the name to see if she could find anyone who would respond to giving Lanai info on who this man was listed as her father. Lanai sent a message to a guy name Aaron and he responded a week later advising he was Lanai's father. Lanai invited him and his family down for the summer so they can get acquainted and Aaron could be in Lanai and her kids' life. They came and spent an entire summer and helped a lot. At the time Lanai was dating a guy name Brandon. Brandon was a great guy and adored Lanai and her children, but he was too clingy and needy. Lanai could not take it anymore and broke up with Brandon. Lanai and her father stayed in touch and he went back to North Carolina. Lanai was in and out of relationships after Brandon until she met a guy while getting her oil changed in Walmart and her friend Ariel was walking to get her baby to drop lower in her stomach. Ariel was pregnant by Lanai's Brother Sean and was due any day. Lanai was standing there minding her own business and notice a guy name Raymond talking to two other people about the military. Raymond had left the store and when Lanai turned around to walk towards her kids Raymond came back in and said, "excuse me ma'am how are you?" Lanai was shocked and in her mind, she was saying, if this little boy don't go somewhere, and her other part of her body was saying, "he can be a one night stand because he military and I probably won't ever see him again. Raymond got Lanai number and then left. When they went their separate ways, Lanai called him and asked him if he wanted to come hangout later that night and he stated sure let me drop my father and brother off. Lanai went home and got the kids settled Raymond was on the way there. Raymond and Lanai sat in the car and talked and then went to the park and had sex multiple times. When they got back to the house they continued to talk until it was time for the kids to go to school. Still in the back of Lanai head she just wanted him to be a one-night stand and never see him again, but before he left her, they both agreed to see each other again. They began to date and made it official and while Lanai started catching real feelings, but Raymond only saw her as a fuck buddy and had multiple sex partners. Lani was not sure of anything anymore because everywhere she searched for someone to love her, she got multiple disappointments. Lanai learned she was looking for love in all the wrong places.

Innocents Taken

Innocents are a virtue. People never know when their personal space can be violated. Lanai was so open and started not to care about herself because she felt why should she care when no one else cared. When Lanai was in her pre-teen age, she was very insecure about the way she looks and felt no one would like her. She always got picked on in school by other kids. They used to call her all types of names such as bald head, ugly, stupid, nerd, etc. At the age of twelve or thirteen she was being touched by one of her family members name Tony. Tony would always say things to her to make her feel like she was beautiful, because she was not getting the attention she wanted from the boys at her school. Tony would always wait until they were alone and talk her into letting him perform oral sex on her and used his fingers to penetrate her vagina. There were times when Lanai felt so uncomfortable, she was scared to say something. Her parents were always gone, and it was just her in the house because her brother/cousin Sean was away in the military. One-night Tony got so bold and came in her room while her dad/uncle John was out doing drugs and her mom would be closing at work and he would touch on her. She was so scared and did not want to do it anymore Lanai told him get out her room before she screams. A couple of weeks after that Tony was then locked up for allegedly molesting a minor boy. Lanai was terrified after that she did not want to even think about letting a guy ever getting close to her again. Every year after he was locked up, he would always send Lanai a birthday card and apologizing for everything for what he uses to do to her. Lanai felt hate, rage, pain, hurt, and disappointed that no one paid any attention to her in her own home to notice anything was wrong. Lanai then got into expressing her feelings threw poetry and music. She already had questions on why her birth parents did not want her and she did not even at the time know who her father was. Lanai held a lot in because she was afraid to confide in anyone and did not know who to trust at that point. As Lanai got older, she learns to become independent and strong on her own because in all reality that is all she had to keep from wanting to cause harm to herself. Lanai was feeling depressed and confused about life in general where she felt she did not deserve to live. The life lanai knew as a child was taken from her when her innocents was taken. Parents words of encouragement pay as much attention to your children as you can because once their innocents are gone, there is no going back.

Road Trips

Lanai first road trip on an airplane was to Maryland. Lanai was working at this Matrix center as a waitress and had to cater a wedding one night. Lanai met these amazing guys that were brothers who performed that night at the wedding. The guys were from Maryland and one of them exchanged numbers with Lanai and invited her to come visit him and record in his studio with him. His name was Melvin and he was so romantic and kindhearted. Lanai had taken a weekend off from work and paid for her airplane ticket and feared her life to get on the airplane. Lanai had never been on a plane before and wanted that experience. Lanai got on the airplane and told the pilot that was her first time flying and so the flight attendant made sure Lanai was comfortable and safe. Lanai had the privileged of riding first class to be closer to the pilot. Lanai got to Maryland to meet Melvin at the airport and head to his house. Melvin got there by the time Lanai got of the airplane and Lanai was nervous as hell. Lanai and Melvin were talking on the phone for 4 months prior to her visit. Lanai thought for sure that Melvin was her man. Lanai had bought Melvin's mother a A.K.A purse and bought Melvin a whole bunch of valentine gifts. Melvin told Lanai that she had to get a room for tonight and then the next night Lanai would have been able to spend the night at his house. Melvin stayed with Lanai at the room for a little while then he had to leave. Lanai took a shower soon as she got to the room and Melvin was already naked in the bed once Lanai got out of the shower. Lanai and Melvin had sex and it really was not worth anything. Lanai thought it was going to be different from any other guy she has been with, but it was not. Melvin wanted his nut and that is exactly all he got. The next day Lanai went to Melvin's house and it was a beautiful home. Unfortunately, it was his parents' home because Melvin could not take me to his apartment because what Melvin failed to mention was that he was engaged. Melvin and Lanai went downstairs to the studio and played around with some music and Lanai heard some of his songs he had recorded with his brothers and they were so amazing. Lanai was shy around Melvin and so she did not really sing in front of him like he wanted her too. Lanai and Melvin then left to get the part that Melvin asked Lanai to get for him. Lanai paid Fifteen hundred dollars for this part for Melvin. Melvin and Lanai then went to a cheesecake factory and had lunch and conversated about the next step in their relationship. Melvin and Lanai then went to his brother's house and played cards and drink some wine. Lanai was getting tired and advised Melvin that she has an early flight in the morning, so she needs to get some rest. Lanai felt like she was being used but wanted to see the best of the situation. Lanai left the next morning and went home. A week later Lanai saw on Melvin's Facebook page all the stuff she had giving Melvin for valentines he gave it to the fiancé and Lanai was so heartbroken. Lanai contacted the female and advised her that she had given all those things to Melvin a week ago when Lanai went to visit him. Lanai flipped out on Melvin and told him to reimburse her the money she had given him. Melvin blocked Lanai and his brothers as well and Lanai never heard from them again. Lanai never took a trip for another man after that because she was tired of men bull shitting her for money. Lanai took road trips with her kids and their friends. Lanai would rent a fifteen-passenger van on her weekend off and take her children to North Carolina to Carowinds and get a hotel and let them get in the indoor pool. Lanai also took her kids to Myrtle Beach one time with Reece and stayed in a condo. Lanai next vacation trip alone was when she met some ppl on this online app called Bigo. There was this girl named chocolate drop and they were the best of friends on the app and off the app. Chocolate drop and Lanai got an Airbnb together and Lanai flew out to California. Lanai had never been to California before and was excited to get there. Lanai had also met these guys on the app named shady, tray way, breezy, and Lboogie and his wife Maria. Lanai drove to Atlanta to catch the plane. Lanai was feeling the guy shady and was planning to see how these LA men get down with the get down if you know wat I mean. Lanai got to the airport and was lost trying to get to her flight on time. She missed her first plane and she thought she was not going to ever get on the plane. Lanai got to her next destination and missed that flight but luckily, she told the people at the airport she needed to catch the first flight that comes available because it was a family emergency. Lanai got on the plane and was in California at twelve thirty when she was supposed to be there at eleven thirty. Lanai got on the bus to get to the rental location to pick up the car and was out of there in like 5 mins. Lanai got into the rental and had Chocolate drop meet her at the Airbnb and then they checked in and unloaded the car with Lanai bags. Lanai had to check in with the police department and then they left to go pick up tray way from his house. After Lanai and chocolate drop picked up tray way, they all went to the store to get some food to cook and drinks. By the time they all got to the room again shady and breezy was already there. Chocolate drop and Lanai started cooking and then Lboogie and Maria had pulled up and we all started drinking and they were smoking. Lanai had went in her room and told shady to come in there with her and they kissed and talked for a little min. Chocolate drop notice we were missing and she came and got me and was like no ma'am come back and join the party. The first night was very lit and Lanai was having the time of her life with everyone. Lanai was tired and was not used to the time frame. Everyone stayed up until about two o'clock pacific time and Lanai and shady shared a bed and chocolate drop and tray way shared a bed and breezy crashed on the couch. Everyone else left and planned to come back the next day. Lanai wanted Shady to make the first move but all he did was just held her and that was very romantic and respectful of him. Shady just wanted to chill and show Lanai a good time and get to know her. Lanai was like on another level, but she also respected the fact that sex was not wat Shady wanted from her. The next morning Chocolate drop and Lanai got up and made breakfast for everyone. Shady asked Lanai to take them somewhere to get some more weed and she said sure. Chocolate drop and tray way stated at the room. Shady and Breezy showed Lanai around LA while they were out, and Lanai got the opportunity to meet Shady's father at his Bike club house. Chocolate drop was calling Lanai trying to find out wat was taking her so long to get back and Lanai advised her that she was coming back soon. They had made a few stops and when they got in the car Shady was like let me get you back before you get in trouble. Lanai, Shady, and Breezy got back to the room and there was this girl name Queen there. Queen was cool with Lanai on the app but when they meet in person it felt like Queen had a problem with Lanai because Queen was interested in Shady as well. Chocolate drop was like Lanai we need some stuff from the store to cook before the stores close and Lanai said ok what we are getting. Lanai went to the store and got some things and we ended up cooking a lot of food that night. Lanai was trying to enjoy her last night with everyone, but they had to end up going home after everyone ate and we cleaned up because Lanai had an early flight in the morning. Lanai took Chocolate drop home first then she took tray way home and shady went home last. Lanai was sad because she was not ready to go home but she had to be at work the next day. Lanai and chocolate drop continued to be friends on the app but shady and breezy did not get on the app as much after that. Shady kept in touch by phone here and there with Lanai but that was it. Lanai met some new people on the app after being kicked out of the access granted family and now Lanai is in the boss kings and queens' family and they rock strong. Lanai name on the app is now BossTastyLuv. Lanai an amazing guy on the app name BossKnowledge which he is in her family on the app. Boss knowledge and Lanai became best of friends and exchanged numbers. Lanai have so much going on in her life with work and relationship wise but whenever she needs someone to make her laugh or lift her up, she always can call on Boss knowledge, Chocolate Drop, and her friend Trina. Road Trips got very slim for Lanai after going to California because the struggle got financial and physically. Lanai also was working more after her premotion at work as SGT. Lanai also was so focus on her relationship that her kids started feeling like she wasn't around as much but in all reality Lanai was just overwhelmed with everything she had going on. Lanai was hurting so much inside from her relationship until it was making her sick inside and very depressed. Lanai had to learn how to channel all of that into her book. Maybe Lanai will get out of her feelings and keep her head up and stay focus and leave her toxic situation.

First Love

Lanai never understood what love she was as was growing up because she did not have anyone to explain it to her. She always thought love meant when someone showed her some attention and made her feel important. Lanai first love was Daniel. Daniel first notice Lanai when they were sitting in burger king where both of their parents worked. One day his mom invited lanai over, and we wrote poetry, played games, and watch movies. Even though they were totally different and saw life at two different aspects they still grew love for one another. Daniel was ill with a blood disorder and got sick all the time. Lanai did not understand what was going on with him and even though they have tried to explain it to her a million times she was afraid to accept it. She was so scared she did not know how to explain to him how it made her feel and did not want to hurt his feelings. Every time it got worse; he did not want Lanai anywhere around to see him in that state of illness. He was embarrassed but she was always concerned about his health. Lanai and Daniel never had a sexual relationship because at this point Lanai was still in school and a virgin. Daniel did not know that Lanai was not sexually active but never asked. Their relationship was up and down after they went to the military ball together. He was never into that type of stuff but only did it because she wanted him to accompany her. That night she was shock because he gave her the most passionate kiss ever. Lanai felt like she was on top of the world after that because that one kiss made her feel like she was cinderella and she never felt that many butterflies in her stomach in her life. A few weeks later Daniel then got sick again and his sister called lanai and asked her to come to the hospital. When Lanai got to the hospital, he was throwing up blood and its terrified Lanai so bad, but she did not let it show. She stood by his side until he went to sleep. She loved him unconditionally and did not know how to tell him. As time go by Daniel and Lanai lost contact for a while and even though they had other relationships there was never a time Lanai never thought about him. She would try and date men with similar traits of Daniel but there were none that could amount to him. One day Lanai got a call from Daniels mom asking if I would help her other son with transportation because we lived right down the road from each other in Columbia and I told her sure. His brother Jeffrey asked me to take him to the laundromat one night and we started talking about how things were in our lives. He then started calling me asking me to take him back and forth to work and to get things from the grocery store. Jeffrey started to be a little annoying at times but nevertheless I got back connect to Daniel again and he invited me over to see him. I went to visit him one day and we went out to eat and then went back to his house and just had a blast talking and reminiscing. Lanai had two kids at the time and still was afraid to have sex with Daniel. Lanai thought in the back of her head that if she slept with Daniel, she would catch that blood disorder disease or end up hurting him in the mist of having sex. She felt he was so fragile, and he could pass out at anytime. If you are in love with someone you should tell them no matter what because tomorrow is not promised, and it will be to late. As time goes by you will hear more about Daniel in my story.

Love Chronicles

Love comes in Lust, secrets revealed, sex, & lies. When you allow someone in your life sometimes it could only be just for that season. Lanai has a high sex drive it was to the point where she felt her body was just what guys wanted. Lanai being using that as her advantage and became very dominate and confident in herself where she would tell men she slept with "just know you're only convenient at this moment, nothing more nothing less don't take it personal." What Lanai also realize was that when having sex with someone its intimate and it will sometimes make her feel less about herself and like she was looked at like a hoe. Lanai love chronicles began when she was broken by her husband. Lanai was so in love with Raymond's body and felt it was all hers and no one could take it from her. Lanai husband Raymond had everything going for him I mean the whole package. He was athletic, nice chested, big dick, and nice firm ass. Lanai loved exploring his whole body in and out. One-night Raymond came home from work and Lanai was in the kitchen cleaning up drinking on some wine. Raymond said bae how was your day and can we go in the room and talk. About what Lanai said to Raymond. I know I've be distance lately, but I think we should try something different in the bedroom. Lanai was always open for trying new things especially if it were to spruce of their sex life. Raymond said to Lanai, "how would u feel if I wanted you to eat my ass," Lanai said, Say What Now," and started laughing. Boy if you do not get out my face with that, and Lanai proceeded to the bedroom with her glass of wine. As they entered the bedroom Raymond said to Lanai can you put on that sexy lingerie I bout you on our anniversary while I jump in the shower? Lanai changed into the lingerie and laid on the bed. Raymond came out the shower and started kissing on Lanai slowly. Lanai already felt things being different because Raymond had never kissed on her so passionately before. Raymond kissed her on the neck then begin sucking on her breast and nipples. He then proceeded to kiss her on inner thighs where he knew was the most sensitive spot on Lanai's body. Raymond had never put his lips this close to Lanai's pussy before. He began to massage his tongue on her pussy, and it felt so good to Lanai she began to exhale. Raymond stayed on her pussy for five mins and Lanai then got up and told Raymond to lay down it was now her turn to please him. Lanai kissed on Raymond's chest slowly and bit & sucked on his nipple as well. For some reason it turned Raymond on when I bit his nipple. Lanai loved Raymond's dick so giving him head was never an issue for her. Lanai sucked on his dick and when she would suck on the head of it and squeezed her lips together on it, it would really drive him crazy. Lanai was always turned on with the moaning sounds Raymond would make as she was giving him head. Lanai began sucking on Raymond balls and the sensitive area under them she realizes then since she was that close to his ass why not. Without hesitation Lanai began licking Raymond's ass and it drove him crazy and made Lanai wetter. After exploring Raymond's body Lanai got on top of his dick and as it slowly went into her wet pussy, she knew it would not be long before he nuts. Lanai pussy would grab his dick and squeeze on it and not even five mins of riding him he would nut, and sex was over. Lanai was so mad because she was close to climaxing, but he was tired and weak after. Lanai got in the shower and by the time she came out of the shower Raymond was knocked out. Lanai said, "Damn, no second round I guess," and she went to bed. Lanai woke up the next morning to find out Raymond had moved out and went to live with one of his frat brothers. Lanai called him and asked him "What the fuck is your problem, and how you going to just up and leave"? Lanai was so blinded by the love she had for Raymond, that she lost herself and allowed him to treat her like she deserved to be disrespected. Lanai left her husband and moved to North Carolina where she was going to start over and focus on what she really wanted which was to start her own restaurant and food truck business. When Lanai first got to North Caroline, she had a mission to get a good job, and save to get her own place and build a future and eventually find true love. Even though Lanai was still married she had been separated from her husband at that point for two years. They were going thru the divorce process, but Lanai did not press the issue because she was still entitled to military benefits. Lanai always wanted to be and Eastern Star, but Raymond made it so hard for her to join any chapter in South Carolina. Lanai was determined to accomplish that journey. One day Lanai was in Walmart in North Carolina where she was grocery shopping and met this lady that was in one of the Chapters there. They exchanged info and Lanai contacted the woman a week later. Lanai was so excited that she was starting in the right path of future greatness. Lanai met with one of the ladies to fill out the application and paid her fee. Lanai had to write a paper stating why she will be a great asset to their organization and how did I learn about them. At the time they were doing open season where you did not have to have a blood line to join. Even though Lanai had a blood line through her husband she did not want his name in anything. Lanai had to go through many steps before finally completing the process and once she was done with the whole process, she was feeling powerful. Lanai had then grown a family of sisterhood where she felt appreciated and loyalty for these amazing group of women. Lanai felt the love and dedication in being involved in the community events. Lanai met this guy at the auto advance store while trying to get her car fixed to be able to go home for the holiday and her church family was also helping her. The guy at the auto place name was Desmond. He really was not lanai type because Lanai was so stuck on Light skin guys, but Lanai decided to change it up. Lanai said, "what's the worst that can happen." Lanai and Desmond begin seeing each other and he advised Lanai that he was married, and Lanai was ok with that. Lanai was under the impression that he was not happy, and he was going to eventually leave his wife. Desmond and Lanai dated for six months and Lanai was starting to catch stronger feelings. Desmond had told Lanai he loved her and was going to go file for the divorce. Lanai then started pushing her papers through for her divorce and was happy that she was going to start a new relationship with Desmond. Lanai then introduced

Desmond to her Mason brothers so he can be in the same Lodge as her and they will have something they could do together. Lanai did not know that Desmond had put his wife information on his paperwork for the application, so everyone knew he was married, and it made Lanai look like a homewrecker. Lanai and Desmond had to stop attending events together but in the back end they still had their sex relationship going. Desmond finally got the papers for the divorce but never filed them. Desmond had advised Lanai that it is a process because they were not separated for a year and they had kids. Lanai was working at waffle house and at this company called Alorica. Desmond and Lanai had to stop seeing each other and go their separate ways because it did not look good for their Chapter. But they remain friends for a while. Lanai met this girl while in training at Alorica. This girl was so sexy to Lanai that she had a hard time focusing on class some days. This girl name was Tamara, she had this soft light skin complexion, with rose red lips, dreamy brown eyes, so when she looked at Lanai it melted her heart. The only downfall with Tamara and Lanai was that Tamara was married and Lanai did not even stand a chance. One day on lunch Tamara and Lanai road together to get lunch and the whole time Lanai was hoping that Tamara would kiss her so she could feel her soft lips. Lanai always felt there was an attraction between them but never pursued it. Lanai got out of training and kept hope to one day get Tamara alone again, but it never happened. Lanai got car was still down, so she had to learn how to drive a stick shift car that she had borrowed from her church member.

Once Lanai got the hang of driving that car, she had to give it back to Mrs. Griffith. Mrs. Griffith was one of the older ladies of the church Lanai attended. Lanai had stopped working at Alorica and waffle house and decided she was ready to go back to South Carolina because things weren't going well in her favor after she felt her dad was taken advantage of her by using all of her food stamps and wanted Lanai to pay him four hundred dollars a month just to live there. Lanai felt she could not save, and it was really draining her, so they had a big fallen out and she packed up her stuff and went back home. As much as Lanai didn't want to leave her family that she had gain with the Eastern Star Chapter she still made it to where she stayed active and made all the events that was allowed with her schedule. Lanai really had a lot going on in her life, where she just had given up on love. She begins just living life with just focusing on her work and her children. She was beginning to be more involved with their sport events and going to games on days she was able to be there. One day she was so tired after work, but she knew she had to go pay for her daughter enrollment for softball. Before Lanai got out her vehicle she said, "fuck a relationship and dating not interested in anything, just wanted to get into a home she was happy with." Lanai wanted to be a homeowner so bad, but it was a struggle being a single parent and trying to fix her credit enough to eventually get to a score where her dreams will come true. When she got out the car and started walking towards the softball field, she was stopped by this guy who she had never seen before. He said to her "excuse me miss can I bother you for a min,"

Lanai said sure what is up? Now in the back of Lanai head she was like, "Why God are you trying to set me up, but damn he is fine." Lanai was at a vulnerable state in her life and wanted to be loved unconditionally. Lanai proceeded to ask him "sir what is your name, and how can I be of assistance to you?" My apologies, ma'am my name is Reece and I just want to know a little bit about you if that's ok." Lanai and Reece exchanged numbers and later that night they conversated. Reece advised Lanai that he was going to huddle house to get something to eat. By this time Reece and Lanai had talked on the phone for two hours. Lanai said ok give me a min and I will meet you there. Lanai got to huddle house and Reece had just walked out. Reece proceeded walk towards Lanai vehicle. When Reece got in Lanai car, she asked him "where is your food?" Reece said, "wrong person cooking so I'm good." Lanai and Reece talked for an hour after he got in the car. Reece left and went home; Lanai guess he thought he was about to get some sex but sadly it was not happening. Reece called Lanai a couple of days later and asked if he could come over and watch a movie. Lanai said, "sure just give me a min to get the kids to bed." Lanai invited Reece in, and they got her laptop a started watching a movie. Reece then took the laptop out of Lanai hand and sat it on the chair and started kissing her. Even though Lanai was trying to wait at least a month before she gave it up, he was determined to get what he wanted. He proceeded to kiss Lanai on all her weak spots starting from her neck to her breast then to her stomach. Reece then pulled her pajama pants off and started sucking on Lanai pussy and licking her clit and caressing her breast as he penetrated her pussy with the other hand. Lanai was so weak she could not help but to let him continue. Lanai could not understand why she was so wet, and it was squirting everywhere. Lanai thought she urinated on this man and was so embarrass. Lanai said wait, Reece I have to use the bathroom feels like I'm peeing." "Reece said, girl you're just squirting, LOL." Reece continued to caress Lanai pussy as she moans passionately. Reece dick went into Lanai pussy slowly and he began to slow stroke Lanai. Lanai and Reece continued having sex until Lanai reached her climax. Reece left after giving Lanai some amazing. Lanai and Reece started dating and having sex every time he stays the night at her place. Three months in of dating Lanai found herself falling in love with Reece extremely fast.

Lanai invited Reece to go with her on a trip to Vegas that she was planning for a while. It was supposed to be an all girls trip, but she could not get a group of women to go. Lanai intentions on this trip was to ask Reece to promise his love to her and to always stay honest with her. Lanai had just received her settlement from her accident and Reece knew that because Lanai had trusted him. Lanai always felt that Reece was to good to be true but could not really see past the love she had for him. Lanai always felt Reece was hiding something just could not put her hands on it, but little do he know Lanai was an investigator. Before leaving to go to Vegas, Lanai had a conversation with Reece Mother Dion in ref to asking Reece hand in marriage. Dion said, "are you sure you want to marry my son and why do you feel that Reece is the one for you?"

Lanai said, “I sure do ma’am because she kept praying about it and asking for signs.” Lanai wasn’t suppose to receive the ring she had got for him until they returned home but it worked out in her favor and she got it in the mail on the day she was leaving for Vegas. Lanai felt that was her final confirmation that it was meant to be. Reece had no clue on what Lanai had in store for him in Vegas. Before leaving for their trip Lanai had gotten a room in Columbia so they could spend some time together the night before traveling. Lanai and Reece, Marsha and Trey went out to eat at Olive Garden and shopping at the mall. Marsha is Lanai niece who was keeping her car while she is out of town and Trey is Marsha’s boyfriend. Reece and Lanai got up early the next morning to catch the airplane and when Lanai booked the flight, she thought they were sitting together but she did not. Lanai ended up sitting in the seat behind Reece and she was terrified of planes and had to hold on to Reece's hand until they were up in the air. When Lanai and Reece landed in Vegas it was late at night and time frame was different from where they were from. They got to their room and got settled in and took a shower and fell asleep. The next day they got up and because their flight was crazy, they ordered room service and stayed in the bed half of the morning. Lanai got up and checked on her kids back home and got dress and then Reece said, "bae lets go out and site see." When Reece and Lanai got downstairs there was a group of people that were on this bicycle ride to club hop and drink at multiple spots and the ride was only twenty dollars. Reece and Lanai met some amazing people from different places on this bike ride and one of the females was eyeing Lanai, but she did not expect anything. Lanai and Reece were so drunk after that ride all they thought about was food and fucking. They got back to the hotel and while lanai prepared herself with the hotel crew to perform to Reece live in front of everyone and propose to him her and one of the ladies from the bike ride went upstairs while everyone else stayed downstairs with Reece. When Lanai got in the elevator the female name Lori came on to her and kissed her. Even though Lanai was about to get engaged she didn't stop Lori from kissing her. Lori and Lanai got upstairs and got to the room and Lanai got the ring out of her suitcase that she had brought for Reece. Lori tried to have sex with Lanai, but Lanai advised Lori that her cycle was on and it cannot down. When they return downstairs

Reece was sitting at the bar drinking more alcohol and Lori friends had kept him company. The hotel manager had the music set up and gave Lanai the mic and Reece was wondering where Lanai was. Lanai came around the corner singing to Reece while Lori and her friends record her singing. When Lanai finished the song, she proposed to Reece on live in front of everyone at the hotel and on social media. Reece then grabbed Lanai and said yes to marrying her and kissed her passionately. Lanai and Reece continued drinking and eating dinner with their new friends they met and then went upstairs to their room. When Reece got in the room his family was blowing up his phone from watching the live footage of the proposal. Lanai and Reece made love that night in their room and Lanai thought for sure that she was going to end up pregnant the way Reece was caressing her pussy with his amazing dick. The next morning Reece and Lanai went exploring the city of Vegas and ended up going to a timeshare presentation. At this presentation they agreed to sign up and have something in both their names as a couple. Lanai never knew anything about a timeshare until that day and Reece explained it to her because he had already had one. Reece convinced Lanai to sign up and made a commitment to have this in both their names. Once they completed the process they went back to their hotel and gambled a little in the casino that was in the lobby area. Lanai felt her luck was not there, so she said she was not about to lose her money. Reece said to Lanai, "baby lets get something to eat and then got relax in our room because it was our last night." Lanai wanted to get in some water while in Vegas, but she never got the chance too. The next morning, they had to catch their plane and the uber cancel on them twice, so they had to share a cab ride with another couple and split the fare. When they got to the airport, they thought they were going to miss their flight, but they made it just in time. But when they got to their second airport, they had missed their flight and ended up having to spend another thousand dollars for more tickets. Lanai was so pissed because it literally was not their fault, they missed the flight. By the time they made it to their destination Lanai niece was supposed to be there to pick them up with Lanai car, but she never showed up. Lanai ended up having to pay a uber to take them home and that ride home was eighty dollars. Once Lanai and Reece got home it was 2am in the morning and

Lanai had to be to work by 6:45am. Lanai had cried so much that morning because it felt like everything was going wrong. Two weeks went by and Lanai and Reece were so happy, and Lanai started asking Reece can we start planning the wedding and setting dates. Once Lanai got the ok from Reece, she started a group chat on WhatsApp with the ladies she wanted to be in her wedding. Lanai had already set the date of the wedding for July 20, 2020 and she had already contacted her aunt Earlene about handling the catering part. Earlene had advised Lanai that she will email her the contract and both parties will need to meet with her to sign the contract with the deposit. Lanai ended up meeting with her aunt Earlene a month Later with Reece and they both agreed that they will sign it and get back with her once they look it over. Another month went by and Lanai and Reece talked about the wedding plans. Lanai would ask Reece over and over if he sure this is what he wanted and he will always say, “yes bae keep doing what your doing.” Lanai sign the contract with the Aunt Earlene for the catering and paid a security deposit of seven hundred fifty dollars that was nonrefundable. Which her auntie had explained to both. Once the catering part was taken care of Lanai and Reece took a trip to North Carolina to meet with her Maid of honor and Matron of honor to try on some wedding dresses. Lanai had tried on like twenty dresses before she found the one, she was love with. Lanai video and prayed over the dress with her Eastern Star sisters Mary and Madison. Reece had come and met them at the crab shack for dinner. Reece seem like he was not all the way there like his mind was somewhere else. When they got to the room and got settled in Lanai proceeded to ask Reece again, "Baby are you sure you're ok with these plans?" "Reece said, "sure bae we're good on everything." The next morning Reece had to leave to handle some business with some of his clients, so Lanai went to Raleigh, North Carolina to pick up her friend Chante and her God child Darius. Lanai and Chante talked the whole ride about her wedding plans and showed her the dress she picked out. Lanai was so tired that she had to let Chante drive halfway back home. When Lanai and Chante pulled up in the yard of Chante's house Lanai told her she will text her soon as she gets home to let her know that she made it safe. Lanai called Reece and asked him if he was coming home tonight and Reece advised Lanai that he was an hour away. Lanai got home and took a shower and by the time she was about to get in her bed Reece was pulling up. Reece and Lanai talked and then fell asleep. Three weeks past and Lanai and Reece were over his sister house drinking and chilling with everyone having a great time. Reece told Lanai he will be back, and he left and went to the store. While out at the store Reece got a call from his child's mother and he went by and picked up his daughter Ralisha not knowing he was getting her mother too Kayla. When Kayla came in, she had a lot of respect, but something was off to Lanai about this girl. Lanai did not let it bother her at first but when Reece had to take Kayla back home that was a problem. Reece got back to his sister Lanisha house to get Lanai but before they left Lanai had a seizure episode and it was trigger from all that uncomfortable situation between Kayla and Reece. Reece had put Lanai in the car to take her and her children home Amir and Omari. When Reece and Lanai got home and got the children out of the car they went in the room and had a long conversation about why he brought Kayla to his sister's house. Lanai felt she was disrespected in so many ways without any warning. After that night of conversating with him Reece got ghost on Lanai without any explanation. Lanai would reach out to his sister Lanisha and Mother Dion. Lanai had called Reece phone for three weeks without an answer. At that point Lanai knew it was over between them and he had other motives with his baby momma Kayla. Lanai continued being close with his family and became best friends with Lanisha. Lanisha and Lanai was inseparable, and they were like two peas in a pod. Lanai finally got in touch with Reece after six weeks of not hearing from him. Reece told Lanai it would be best if we be just friend because Lanai was to good of a woman for him to drag down. Lanai was so heartbroken until she could not breath and had relapse where she had to go to counseling. And weeks after weeks she would have a seizure episode. Lanai went to Lanisha house one day just over there chilling and talking and then Reece and Kayla came in like a couple and that's when Lanai was so pissed to the point where she wanted to shoot both of them. Lanai had another seizure and at this time Kayla was the one who had to help her through it and then Reece came in and assisted, when in all reality the both of them was the cause of her episodes. Lanai got to point where she had to limit her visitation to Lanisha house because she was not ok with Reece and Kayla relationship. It took Lanai a year to get back to her normal self which that was still a question mark because Lanai did not know who she really was. Lanai became confident about herself once she completed multiple sessions with her counselor which was also her best friend Melody. Melody was only an hour and a half away from Lanai but both of their schedules were so busy where they communicated mainly through text, facetime, or phone calls. Lanai knew that Melody was never going to confuse their friendship with business when it came to getting Lanai to understand her worth and how much more important, she was. Melody Knew Lanai had been going through so much in every relationship she ever was in because it seems to become a pattern of wrong choices of men. Lanai took a year off from dating and just had sex with people. Lanai started to feel like sex was a way of not even thinking or feeling anything. Lanai slept with men that were married mainly to keep from having strings attached. Before sleeping with them Lanai would always let them know she do not do the cuddling, sleepovers, kissing, sucking dick, or threesomes. Lanai made it very clear that she was toxic and that they will catch feelings but do not because it will never be more than just sex. Lanai got to a point where sex got boring to her with men until she took a break after being active with them for 5 months. Lanai went 8 months without having sex with a man and realized that she was interested in dating girls again. What people did not know about Lanai was that she always knew she liked girls but was only doing what she felt was appropriate to her family.

Lanai was always the type to please everyone else in her family even it was against her own happiness. Lanai was always in desperate search of attention and Love that she never found that in any man. Lanai was working back at the Sheriff department as a dispatcher, deputy, investigations, and she was also a federal agent. Lanai kept herself so busy after her break up with Reece and want to excel her horizons. She had been back with the agency for a year at this point when she started noticing this girl, she was interested in. This girl was a deputy that was with the county but when she got to know the girl and her actions, she just wanted to be friends with her. Her name was Janay and her and Lanai became the best of friends. Everyone would warn Lanai about this girl, but she felt she needed to be friends with her to guide her and show that she was not nothing like wat people thought about her. Janay had been a trifling backstabbing bitch multiple times to Lanai, but she did not learn that Janay was not ever in her best interest until shit the fan. Lanai had taken Janay daughter Kiara in while she went to the academy and whenever Janay needed Lanai she was always there. Lanai had told Janay that she had a crush on her, but she would never try Janay because she was wreck less with her life and Lanai never trusted to go beyond just friendship. Lanai had also noticed this other girl who worked for the EMS department but at the time this girl was in a relationship with someone. This girl name was Shay. Shay was a whole stud but reminded Lanai of her crush Tamara in North Carolina. Once again Shay was bright light skin, dread head, with a smile that will brighten your day every time. Lanai notice her multiple times but respected that she had a relationship. One day Shay came in dispatch to train and spoke to Lanai and it shocked the hell out of Lanai. When Lanai and Shay connected eyes, Lanai knew it was a possibility to get to know Shay on another level. Shay had Lanai had exchanged info and was texting for that week they worked together. Shay told Lanai that she has been watching her for awhile, but she was in a relationship with this girl name Bree that worked with EMS first then started working with the Sheriff department with Lanai. Lanai told Shay she was watching her as well but just respected their relationship. Lanai was smiling from ear to ear to know that this could be a path of greatness to come. That weekend came and Shay called Lanai and was like hey can I come spend time with you for a little while if you do not have anything planned. Lanai said, "sure that's cool I didn't have anything planned." Lanai knew that questions were going to spark when Shay came around and she did not know how her kids were going to take it. Also, Lanai did not expect anything to happen because she was on her cycle that weekend which sucked because Lanai wanted something to happen. Shay Called Lanai when she was outside, and Lanai told her to come in. Shay Came in and Lanai was laying across her bed working on her book. Lanai told Shay she could have a seat on the bed, so Shay laid down. They were face to face and Shay just kept looking at Lanai as she worked on the book. Shay asked Lanai can she read some of her book and Lanai said, "sure but its emotional." Shay started reading the book and she was so shocked by how emotional it was. Lanai then asked Shay if she wanted something to drink or eat. Shay said, "no I'm good, but you can give me your hand so I can read you." Lanai was so nervous around Shay because Lanai did not know wat to expect. Lanai was shy when it came to looking Shay or anyone at that matter straight in the eye. Lanai introduced Shay to her kids and then Shay phone rings. Shay ignored the call and Lanai asked Shay to ride with her to her friend/sister's house so they could meet. When Lanai and Shay got there, they begin talking and watching a movie with Lanisha and her children. While watching the movie, Shay had kiss Lanai unexpectedly. Lanai felt butterflies in her stomach because it felt so right. Lanai asked Shay wat was that for and can they take a picture on snap. Shay said, "sure and Lanai took the picture and then posted it. Shay and Lanai left and went back to Lanai's house and they started watching a movie. Lanai and Shay fell asleep in the mist of watching the movie. The next morning Lanai woke up not expecting Shay to still be here and Lanai turned over and was like wat the fuck. Shay and Lanai was going off at the same time. Shay ex-girlfriend was calling, and my supposedly best friend Janay was calling Lanai phone. Shay answers her phone and Bree asked Shay, "YOU FUCKIN LANAI?" Shay asked Bree, "Wat are you talking about?" Lanai answered her phone and Janay said, "what are you doing today because Kiara and I was on the way to you.? Lanai told her she had plans to take the kids to the water park and she was busy this weekend. Janay offered herself and Kiara to come along and Lanai was trying to hurry up and leave but by the time she went to walk out her door, Janay and Kiara was already here. Everyone piled up in Lanai car and head to water park. Lanai did not know why Janay wanted to just come and hang out suddenly. Janay had told Lanai that Bree called her and told her about the picture Shay, and I had taken on snap. Janay were playing two sides of the field because she had another motive. When Lanai, Shay, Janay, and all the kids got back from the water park everybody decided they wanted seafood for dinner. We went to the store and shopped for all the groceries. Shay was uncomfortable with coming my mom house so her and Janay sat outside on the porch while Lanai was slaving over the stove for everybody. Lanai thought everything was good with Shay, but little did Lanai know her so called friend Janay was working her evilness on getting Shay for herself. Shay and Janay went to the store by themselves for Lanai and then came back. Lanai pulled Janay to the side and told her how much she had like Shay and wanted to see where it goes with her. Janay knew how much Shay meant to Lanai, but wat Janay wants Janay gets even if it hurts the next person. Janay left after she ate, and Shay and Lanai went back to her house and started talking again. Shay asked Lanai about her past relationships at the Sheriff department and Lanai was kind of confused where that came from. Lanai was honest with her and told Shay about her past but did not expect that to change how they felt about one another. Lanai and Shay fell asleep after that conversation and woke up the next morning on the same page. Shay kissed Lanai and her boys Amir and Omari before she left and told Lanai she will call her once she got home. Lanai and Shay talked on the phone and Shay asked Lanai again if she was single and Lanai said, “yes why you ask?” Shay just said, “no reason, just asking.” Monday came and Lanai felt she had an amazing weekend with Shay, and everything was going to be good. Shay called Lanai and told her a lot of shit had happen and they needed to talk. At this point Lanai did not know wat to expect and was upset because she did not know wat happen or why Shay was not telling her anything. Janay had everyone in Lanai and Shay business about this past weekend. What Lanai did not know is that her and Shay could not have a relationship at the department because it was against policy. In all reality that policy only applied to certain employees because like Lanai said in the beginning Bree and Shay were together before

Lanai and Shay started talking. No one seem to have a problem when Bree and Shay was dating. Bree and Lanai had tension between them when all this confusion went on. Shay told Lanai that they could not be friends anymore and they needed to go their separate ways. Lanai was so devastated because she had really liked Shay. Lanai came out to her family for this girl because she wants to see where it went and eventually start a future together. Shay stopped talking to Lanai and two weeks later Shay and Janay were in a relationship. At the time Lanai did not know that they were together until Janay came to the office one day for paperwork and before she left, she stopped down on the EMS side to see Shay. So, when Lanai saw them all hugged up and in love with one another, Lanai felt like both had stabbed her in her heart a million times. Lanai reached out to Shay to check on her and asked her why she left me for my suppose to be best friend, and Shay told Lanai that she need to stop reaching out because her girlfriend didn't want me having contact with her. Shay unfriend Lanai on snap. Lanai texted Janay and told her off and told her to never say anything to her again and asked her how she could do that to me. Janay said, "it wasn't intentional things just happen." A week after Lanai told Janay off Janay continued to try and talk to Lanai and Lanai advised her to stop contacting her and blocked her. Lanai was so torn because it was close to being her birthday and she was so hurt. So, Lanai downloaded this lesbian app and started to connect with new people. Lanai connected with this girl on the app name Lex. Lex was sexy to Lanai. Lanai started chatting with Lex and they exchanged numbers. Lanai asked Lex wat she did for a living, and she said, I am an Assistant General Manager at Taco Bell in Columbia. Lex asked Lanai wat type of work she did, and Lanai said she worked for Law Enforcement State and Federal. Lex was like I fear you ma'am lol. Lanai said why and Lex was like because you are the Law and me and the Law do not get along. Lanai asked Lex if they could meet and Lex advised sure when. Lanai went to Lexington where Lex lived a week later and picked her up and brought her back to the house. Lex and Lanai connected that day physically and mentally. Lanai did not expect things to go the way they did. The way Lex made Lanai felt when she kissed her lips, cheek, neck, hand, and back was like very passionate. Lex was trying to make Lanai fall deep in love with her sexually. Lex and Lanai were in the room alone at Lanai house and Lex started kissing Lanai on her breast and caressing them softly. Lex then worked her way down to Lanai belly button and then down between her thighs and Lanai knew that was one of her weak spots. Lanai had not had sex for seven months, so she was vulnerable. Lex began to caress Lanai pussy with her tongue and Lanai was mesmerized and was not expecting Lex to be amazing with her tongue movement. Lex then inserted two fingers in Lanai pussy while still sucking on her clit and fingering her. Lex notice Lanai was moaning and enjoying her Lex then inserted another finger in Lanai pussy. Lanai was longing for an orgasm for a while now and Lex was determined to make that happened. Lex knew exactly where Lanai g-spot was and hit it right on the money. Lanai had not squirted like that since

Reece. Right then and their Lanai knew that Lex and she was meant to be together. Lex was not the type to let Lanai touch her or please her. Lex was more the pleaser than anything and Lanai was ok with that. In the back of Lanai mind after that great oral sex moment, Lanai was thinking why she would let anyone else can steal Lex from her. Lanai had just lost Shay to Janay and was not about to let that happen again. Lanai would talk to Lex every day and want to see her just as much. Lex was a handful, and had a lot going on in her life. Lex was still living with her ex-girlfriend and their three boys and daughter. Even though Lex and Lanai were in a relationship with one another Lex wanted Lanai to be patient with her and give her time to get out of her situation. Lanai was understanding when it came to that but at the same time did not agree with how everything was when it came to spending time together. The first two months of Lex and Lanai being together everything was ok; it was not the best, but it was a process. Lex told Lanai that she still cared for her ex-girlfriend, which was named Kandace, but did not want to be with her. Lanai was kind of confused like how she expected me to take that. Lex had told Lanai that she put a down payment on a house for Kandace and she will not leave to move in the house. So, at this point Lanai was like well put her out and get a restraining order if she will not leave. Honestly, it is more to the story then Lex wanted to tell. Lanai was starting to be impatient with her situation, so she kept expressing her feeling to Lex and it stated making Lex more and more distant away from her. Lex would stop coming to see Lanai, so Lanai started making more trips to see Lex because Lanai was starting to feel like she was losing Lex. Lanai friend Chante had asked Lex to have Lanai come pick her up after work because she had planned a surprise birthday party that night at Lanai house. Lanai did not know what was going on. Lex kept telling Lanai to drive home and do not worry about it. Lanai and Lex pulled up to the house and all of Lanai kids and her friends and family was there to surprise her on her special day. Lanai kissed Lex and thanked everyone for everything they had done for her. Lanai was having the time of her life and got so drunk until she tried to rape Lex that night while everyone was still there. Lanai finally got Lex alone in the room and got sick from all the alcohol she had consumed. Lanai jumped up out of the bed and went to the bathroom and threw up. Lex asked

Lanai if she was ok and Lanai said yes. Lanai then brushed her teeth and came out of the bathroom to get back to kissing on Lex, but she was knocked out when Lanai came out. The next morning Lanai had to be to work and she woke up late and told Lex to get up they had to go. Lex and Lanai got to her job it was like seven thirty when Lanai was supposed to be there by six forty-five. Lex sat in the car while Lanai went into work to relieve her person and apologized for being late. Lanai was sick out of this world and did not want to be there at all. Lanai was trying to figure out a way to leave work early because she was still sick from the night before. Lex was knocked out in the car when I went out to check on her. Lanai wanted to get off early to continue spending time with Lex. Lex sister was supposed to meet them halfway, but Lanai really could not leave after being late to meet Lex sister. Lex sister name is Angela and so Angela came all the way to Lanai job to pick Lex up. Lex and Angela left Lanai job and Lanai told Lex she would like to see her later if possible. By the time Lex got back to Lexington Lanai had found someone to cover the rest of her shift for her. Lanai was in and out of the bathroom because she did not have anything to eat since she threw up the food from the night before. Lanai felt after her birthday celebration that things would get better between her and Lex and thought Lex would open more to her. Lex started having more time for her friends and going to the strip club and making less time for Lanai. Lex got sick and she thought she had Covid because that's wat the result came back as but it was pneumonia. Lanai got all her kids tested and even her cousin. Lanai daughter Patience and Cousin Trevon ended up having the Virus. Lanai was on vacation for a week from her job and was supposed to go out of town that week, but Lanai ended up having to take care of her daughter and cousin. Lanai had received a gift for her birthday from her friend name Trina. Trina had bought Lanai some Roses and gave her all together like two hundred dollars. Lanai had told Trina she did not have to, but she was insisting on doing it anyway which Lanai really loved. Lanai ended up having to call her supervisor to advised that two people had the Virus in her home, and they advised her that she had to stay home for two weeks. The two extra weeks Lanai wanted Lex to come down so Lanai could have taken care of her as well. Lanai body was so broken down because she was sick because she could not see Lex or spend time with her. Lanai felt something was wrong between her and Lex and did not know exactly wat it was. Lanai took care of the kids until their results came back clear. While taking care of her cousin which was not her job because he had a mother that should have been doing it. Trevon mother had so much to say about Lanai because Lanai was so tired and told his mom that he needs to come home and she needed to take care of him. Instead of Malinda getting her son Trevon, she had her family send food and stuff to Lanai house for him. Malinda was saying that Lanai was not doing was supposed to be doing for her son and that she was treating Trevon like he was a disease. When Lanai was the only one who was doing for Trevon making sure he had everything he needed. At the same time taking care of her daughter Patience and her other Children. Lanai was dealing with so much to the point where she just wanted to disappear. Lex was not giving Lanai the attention she needed and wanted, and Lanai kids were about to drive her crazy. Lanai asked Lex to come down one day and they went to taco Tuesday with some of Lanai friends and coworkers. Lex and Lanai had so much fun and she really enjoyed that restaurant. After Lanai and Lex left the restaurant, they went back to Lanai house and started talking. Lex had to many drinks and started being aggressive with Lanai and started saying things about Lanai that was not true. Then when Lanai told Lex she did not have take this verbal abuse she walked out the house. Lex came after her and started grabbing her apologizing and said she did not mean any of those things she said to Lanai.

Lanai was scared out of her life because she did not know wat to expect and why Lex flipped on her after they had just had a great time wit Lanai friends. Lex has not been back to Lanai house since that night, she stopped coming. Lex situation got extremely complicated with Lanai where she was honestly tired of Kandace having control on how Lex moved. Lex had already met Lanai kids and Lanai could not understand when she was going to be able to meet Lex kids. Lex told Lanai that they needed to talk about something that happen while she was sick. Lanai was not prepared to hear any bad news. Lex had told Lanai when she was sick, she went to the strip club with some friends and a stripper was all over and kissing on her and after that she went to the stripper house and ate some food. Lex said they never done anything just that night the stripper just was aggressive with kissing her. Lanai was so hurt and broken because she could not understand why Lex would allow someone so nasty to kiss her. Lanai asked Lex, “you didn’t love me enough to stop her,” Lex then gave her some bullshit answer, “Bae I was Drunk.” Lanai said, “That doesn’t excuse the fact that it happened.” Lanai felt like Lex was not ready for nothing real. Months went by without Lanai seeing Lex and spending time with her. Lex had told Lanai that there was an event coming up for Kandace daughter in North Carolina and how would she feel if she went. Lanai was not feeling that at all. Lanai said, “Lex lets make a trip out of it because my father stays close to that same area.” Lex did not want Lanai to go because she felt it will cause drama between her and Kandace. At that point

Lanai felt like Lex was still not telling her the full story about her and Kandace. Lanai felt like Kandace was still in the picture as Lex main and Lanai was her go to when she did not want to deal with Kandace. Lanai was tired of Lex not being honest with her and keep asking Lanai to please be patient. Lanai was being more than patient, and everyone was saying Lanai you were allowing less then she deserved from Lex. Lanai was so blinded by love that once again she was allowing Lex to take advantage of her kindness and love. Lex was not the type to buy things or spoil Lanai and even though Lanai was a giving a person she wanted to show Lex how much she meant to her. Lex ended up going to North Carolina with Kandace and spending the whole time up there with Kandace family and the kids. Lanai was off that weekend and wanted to spend it wit Lex but did Lex care, not at all. Lex and Lanai had been arguing for months and Lanai knew Lex birthday was coming up. Even after Lex was disrespectful and did not care how Lanai felt she kept that same nonchalant attitude as she knew Lanai was not going anywhere. In Lanai head she was like maybe a night of love and affection is what they needed to make things better between them. Lanai called Lex sister Angela to pick up some rose pedal, a card, and candles. Lanai children and niece had done a poster board for Lex and decorated the hotel room that Lanai had book for Lex birthday. All week Lanai was asking Lex wat she had planned for her birthday and Lex said she did not know. So, with her saying she did not know, Lanai felt this was something could do special for Lex. Everyone that cared for Lanai and

Lex chipped in and help. Lanai was done setting up the room for there romantic night and had everyone wait until she got back from Lex job. Lanai had planned a whole concert for Lex at her job. Lanai got out of the car while Lex coworkers and Angela recorded Lanai singing to Lex. After Lanai had sing to Lex, they kissed and chilled in the parking lot for a while. Then Lex and Angela went to the side and talked while Lanai sat in the car already feeling like Lex was not going to leave with her to go back to the room. Lex then came back to the car to talk to Lanai and asked Lanai, “wat is you about to do when you leave here?”. Lanai said, “that all depends on you”. Lanai handed Lex the key to the room and told her the room number that she will be in. Lex never said if she was coming or not. At that point Lanai was done with all the games and the bullshit.

Lex knew that after that night she was not going to have Lanai in her life and things were going to change. Lanai got back to the room and cleaned up all the decorations and cried all night in that nice king size bed alone. Lex continue to text Lanai and that did not help at all because when Lanai asked Lex why she could not come she said she just could not and that it was complicated. Right then and their Lanai knew that Lex had chosen her situation over Lanai and that broke Lanai's heart. Angela apologized so much for Lex that night until it was like she felt so bad for Lanai. Angela had got a room down the hall from Lanai by herself as well cause she wanted to be close to Lex and Lanai, but again it was only Lanai. Lanai did not go to sleep that night until three o'clock because could not sleep and was crying. Lanai finally went to sleep and woke right back up at six thirty thinking it was all a dream and Lex was going to be next to her and it was not. Lanai just laid in the bed until about eight and then she went to Angela room to borrow her charger to charge her phone. Lanai then laid back in the bed until it was close to check out time. Angela came to Lanai room about eleven to let Lanai know she was about to leave and go home. Angela went downstairs to check out and they would not let her without Lanai. Lanai then got up and got dress so they could leave at the same time. When they checked out Lanai was not ready to go home, she decided to go get something to eat at her favorite restaurant Olive Garden. Lex had text Lanai phone and at first Lanai was not responding but then she decided to respond. Lex had asked Lanai wat she was doing, and Lanai responded eating. Lex asked where so Lanai shared her location and told her she has thirty minutes to get there. Lex then said, “I don’t have a way there” and I advised she better ask her sister Angela. Lex asked Lanai were they still on for today so she can make it up to her for not showing up last night, and Lanai said on for wat and no we are not. Lex said her favorite thing, “BET”. Lanai then got in her car and was about to leave Columbia when Lex said, “why did you do all of that for me I didn’t asked for that” and she made Lanai feel like she had done something so wrong, when in all reality Lex shouldn’t have made no plans but for her girlfriend. Lanai responded back to wat Lex had said and said, “You’re right my bad, cool.” Lanai left the restaurant and headed back home. The whole ride home Lanai was broken and cried and felt like she could not breathe because that was the last strike for her to do anything else for Lex. Lanai got home and got a call from Trina her friend and she invited Lanai over. Lanai niece Marsha was over her house and had agreed to keep the twins and help them with school. Lanai came and packed her clothes and stayed at Trina house all week. Lanai was still so upset wit Lex that she needed something to distract Lanai from everything she was dealing with. Even though she was mad at Lex she still communicated with her thru text messages and Lex even called her sometimes. Lanai would always say she is done with Lex and then Lex would say something to make her feel like she is really trying. Lanai has such a forgiving heart and lost of confidence in herself to where she does not want to be alone, so she lowered her standards for Lex. Lanai had to get back on her Mother A game and she knew just the person to call to get her back to that Boss Status of not caring about anyone else feelings but her own. Lanai had called her ex-husband Raymond and told him everything that she had going on. Raymond went in on Lanai and sent her memes and all type of encouraging things. Lanai planned her weekend accordingly. Friday Lanai had planned to go to sleepy hollow with her cousins and Lex, but she already figured Lex was not going to show up like always. Lanai never went and ended up spending the night with Trina with her boys Amir, Omari, & David Jr. Once again Lex had disappointed Lanai. Lanai friend Trina said, "FUCK HER LANAI, SHE DOESN'T DESERVE YOU PERIODT." Trina is such a Loyal Friend to Lanai that she allows Lanai to come crash at her spot anytime. Trina likes girls too, but she respects our friendship and knows about Lex. Saturday morning came and Lanai had to wake up by six thirty to be in manning for her daughter Patience meeting for upward bound and because Trina didn't mind she told Lanai that she would drive her there and the boys could stay her until they returned. Trina and Lanai got up Late and got her baby Emily dressed and the twins and got to manning by seven fifty-five. Patience was waiting on her mother Lanai and Lanai took the twins to her mother/aunt Betty who lived next door to Lanai. Lanai advised Betty to watch the kids while she attended this meeting for Patience, and she will pick the boys up after. Lanai had left David and Trina nephew Noah at the house by themselves because they were older. Lanai and Trina had only gotten maybe three hours of sleep tops the night before, so they were beat. Trina and

Emily waited in the car while Lanai went inside of the meeting that was not worth getting up for. Honestly that meeting could have been handle by an email, “said Lanai.” Patience had to stay there until three o’clock, but Lanai meeting was over by nine. Lanai got in the car and went back to Betty house to pick up Amir and Omari her twin boys. Lanai and Trina headed back to Columbia and went and got some food for them and the kids. Lanai had a whole day planned for her and the kids. She wanted Trina to be involved but she is a home body and not really a people person when she does not really know them. Lanai had to take the twins Amir and Omari to their grandmother Mrs. Daniels. Mrs. Daniels and Lanai really did not care for one another, but she swallowed her pride and asked her to keep the twins. Even though Lanai knew Mrs. Daniels was going to come out of her mouth sideways at her Lanai still was respectful to her. Lanai got the boys to Mrs. Daniels by three thirty and left to head to Charleston for her Godson birthday party with David Jr. Lanai arrived at Chuck E Cheese by four thirty and when Lanai walked in Chante and her best friend John looked at Lanai and said, "Girl I was just talking shit about you wasn't coming." Lanai told Chante she was not about to miss her baby birthday. Lanai Saturday was full of all kind of events. Lanai and David Jr left the party around six thirty-seven o'clock and headed to Orangeburg to a gathering with some of her Co-workers. Lanai got to her friend house in Orangeburg by eight o'clock. Lanai friend name is Nicole which she had just left dispatch for better opportunities and wanted to celebrate with a group of us. So, it was Nicole,

Latoya, Kiesha, & Shardae. Nicole sons were there as well name Jamir and Jaquez. Jamir was with the vibes, but Jaquez was in chill mode with his girlfriend. When Lanai first got there, she had her son David with her, and Nicole told Lanai that he is more than welcome to sit in the tv room. Latoya, Shardae, and Kiesha told Nicole to give Lanai that white milky tequila and a strawberry tequila and when Lanai took both shots, she felt like she was taking medicine it was so nasty. Lanai had so much fun that night with her co-workers and that's exactly wat Lanai needed to keep from showing the pain she was really feeling inside from her relationship with Lex. Lanai did not realize how much her relationship was affecting her physically, mentally, emotionally, and sexually. Lanai was so hooked on Lex until it was not real. Lanai could not understand wat Lex had on her and why Lanai could never let her go. Lanai needed to get to a place where she realizes she was the side chick. Lanai wanted to believe she was the main and, in all reality, she was in denial.

Wrong Choices

Lanai wrong choices began when she allowed her family to determine how she was going to live her life. Lanai always wanted to do wat was right for everyone else instead of herself. Lanai knew since third grade that she was interested in girls but because she was in a family who only believed that women should be with men and men should be with women, Lanai did just that. Lanai had always wanted approval for the things she did in her life. Lanai life as an adult was when she was sixteen and had to start working at The Shrimper and she had to work to get the things she wanted in life to fit in at school. Lanai always wanted attention but was not getting the attention and love she wanted from home, so she searched for it in all the wrong places.

Lanai next in counter of wrong choices was when she allowed herself to get side tracked from doing the right thing the night she went to the park to have sex at eighteen with someone who she thought loved her and really didn't. Lanai got pregnant the first time she had sex. Lanai waited three months to tell her mother who was already busy with work to even pay her attention. Lanai got so much attention once everyone found out she was pregnant with her first child, but again it was not the attention Lanai wanted. Lanai family judged her for having a child her last year in school and told Lanai she was following in her mother footsteps. Lanai loved her daughter Lashay so much and felt she was going to get the love she was longing for from this innocent little person who did not asked to be here. Lanai mother Betty quit working to take care of Lashay so

Lanai could finish school but that's when Lanai had to grow up even more and start working at the Detention Center. Lanai wrong choices continued with every man she ever dated and all she was ever good for in the eyes of men was having babies. Every man she had a child with she thought they loved her and wanted to build a future but none of them amounted to wat she wanted. Lanai was in over her head with taking care of everyone else and her kids. Lanai tried running away from her problems by moving from place to place to start over and there was always a stumble in her pathway. With all the wrong choices Lanai made in her life she never stops striving to prove herself being worthy of greatness and excellence. Lanai had accomplished so many great things in her life but no one notice the good that Lanai did always say the bad in her and judged her like they judged her birth mother when she had to give her up. Lanai worked hard to be in the position that she is in at her job. Lanai was determined to show her family that just because she had bad relationships, and wrong choices in her life nothing was going to stop her from being the best parent she could be for her children. Lanai struggled with college classes online but still did it. Lanai struggled with keeping up with her bills, but Lanai never showed that she could not handle it or maintain. Lanai was a parent, private investigator state and federal, dispatcher, and a motivational speaker. Even though Lanai family looked down on her because of her wrong choices, she was not going to let them bring her spirit down. Wat people fail to realize is that no one is perfect and everyone has made bad choices once in their lives but at the end of the day, it's up to them to make the best of it and change the pattern. Lanai was so strong minded and regardless of wat she had going on in her life whether it was relationship or business she never gave up on being great and showing her kids how to be great. When Lanai made the choice to come out about being a lesbian to her children and her family, she did not care wat anyone thought or how it would make them feel. Lanai was done worrying about the next person and was happy with herself for being able to be herself without feeling guilty. Lanai children do not care, and they accept it with no problem, and everyone can really kiss Lanai ass at the end of the day because her happiness is more important than wat anyone can think or say. Lanai has come to terms with her family not accepting her being a lesbian.

Lanai can honestly say maybe she has made some wrong choices but her being who she is was not one of them. Lanai journey will be very interesting further along in the book so just wait and see how things change in Lanai's life.

Rebuild

Rebuild comes with motivation, energy, determination, and dedication. Lanai motivation to rebuild her life and goals were her children. Lanai always told her children that the word “Can’t” was not in her vocabulary. As many time people told Lanai that she cannot do this and she cannot do that, Lanai made it her business to try and accomplish it. Sometimes it worked in Lanai favor and sometimes it did not, but it never stopped Lanai. Lanai want to be a singer all her life and she never gave up on trying to pursue her dreams. Lanai would go to North Carolina sometimes to the studio at her cousin Devin house and record her music. Lanai and Devin were the closest and his brother Meechi. Devin and Meechi were more like brothers to Lanai then anyone. Meechi and Lanai both had five children with sets of twins. Lanai felt like Meechi jinks her with the twins. Lanai tried multiple times to rebuild a relationship with her brother Sean multiple times, but it seems like every time he got in a relationship and Lanai and his girlfriends had issues, he would always side with them. Lanai tried to rebuild a relationship with her mother/aunt Betty, and they were good most of the time until Lanai felt like even though she was not her biological daughter she treated her like an outsider. Rebuilding a life of greatness and accomplishments comes with time and dedication and that's exactly wat Lanai had. Lanai wanted to be complete and happy that she was not going to let anyone, or anything get in the way of that. Lanai wants a house where she can make it feel like a home that she never had. Lanai wants to love someone who loves her just as much and her children. Lanai wants to be set in a career that she is happy with and do not have to live paycheck to paycheck. Lanai thought once she found someone who was a team player and wanted the same lifestyle that she wanted that they would be a powerhouse that was untouchable. When Lanai met Lex, she felt Lex was the one she wanted to start a new beginning a life with. Lex would ask Lanai to marry her, quit her job and let me take care of you and Lanai would be like, "girl you crazy" "I Know You Fuckin Lying." Lex was not ready for wat Lanai was ready for because Lex never showed the commitment that Lanai was longing for. Lex never made the effort to get out of her situation that she had with her ex living with her and making time for Lanai. Lanai never asked for much from Lex

Lanai just wanted time and for Lex to give her the same energy she was giving. Lanai went over and beyond to prove her love to Lex, but because Lex had the mindset that Lanai would never leave her, she felt she could continue with the foolery and Lanai will always be there. Little did Lex know that once Lanai got to that point of not giving a fuck about how she felt and wat Lex may have thought, Lanai would keep it moving like Lex never existed. There were plenty of times where Lanai children felt like Lanai was neglecting them because Lanai was putting to much time in trying to spend with Lex. Lanai children started making her feel like she was never there, and Lanai twins would always ask why Lex have not came back or bought their shoes she had promise them. Lanai was big on her children feelings and know that they have done been through so many disappointments that she was not going to allow Lex to do that to them. One thing she never tolerated was someone saying they going to do something and not following through with it. Lanai always believe that your word is your bond and if you fall back on your word then nothing else you say will ever matter. Lanai always told anyone she ever delt with that "I will give you all of me and my trust in the beginning, but if you break that trust you will have to go through hell and high waters to gain it back." Lanai has rebuilt so many relationships and friendships from her bigo friends and family until she felt like the people, she saw on the regular was as fake as the weave they had in their hair. Lanai has friend on bigo that she calls brown suga and she is from Chicago. Brown Suga was an older woman who knew exactly wat she wanted in life and always gave Lanai some good advice. Brown Suga did not like the fact that Lex was taking advantage of Lanai good heart and Lanai would be stressing over it. Lanai and Brown Suga could talk about every and anything without the other placing judgment on anything. When Lanai first came to the bigo app there were a few that she trusted and a few she wanted to choke the living shit out of but she never lost character on the app. Lanai, Brown Suga, Chocolate drop, Boss Knowledge, and a few others were the main crew that no matter wat went on-on the app they still had each other back outside of the app. Lanai had rebuild her life with a new family and friends from the bigo app and wouldn't trade anyone of them for nothing. Even though Lanai could not rebuild her life and future with Lex at this time, who is to say that Lex will not grow up and be the woman Lanai needs her to be later in life. One thing Lanai can say though is “Lex bet not wait to long to get her Muther Fuckin life together, because ,Lanai is a bad Bitch and she don’t wait for no one to get on board PERIODT POOH.” In the words of the baddest, “YOU BETTA ASK ABOUT ME.”

House Hunting

Today is a new day and Lanai is looking for a house she can eventually call a home. Lanai had never really lived on her own without a man or woman living with her. Lanai is making it her duty to Rebuild her life with a home of her own where no one can say they helped her get where she is at. Lanai always had a pride issue about herself but let her tell it she did not. Whenever Lanai would move out to try to be on her own, she never really took her daughter with her because they always wanted to stay with their nana. Which at times that was a plus because her daughters got tired of switching school and they were older so they would have to get new friends. New moves were never fun for Lanai when she was growing up so she knew that her children would not like it either. Lanai boys always went wherever she went because they were younger and just really starting in school. Lanai is in the process of house hunting and trying to purchase a home on her own. Lanai do not want many to know just yet until the paperwork was completely done. Lanai was always told keep your moves to yourself, because the next person you tell will probably be the one destruction of your greatness. Lanai always want to move away from her family because she felt like they always drained her energy and always wants to control her every move. Lanai currently lives next door to her mother/aunt Betty and even though it was convenient for her with the kids having a place to go while Lanai worked, Lanai felt smothered and felt she had no privacy. Lanai oldest daughter did not live with her she stayed with Betty, but Lanai felt her daughter was out to destroy her life when it came to her relationships. Lanai felt like Betty was sometimes using Lanai daughter LA 'Shay against her. Lanai found herself closer to her daughter Patience, her niece Marsha and Liliana, more than her oldest daughter LA 'Shay. Lanai could tell her kids anything without it getting back to her mother except LA 'Shay. LA 'Shay was the type of child who thought she was grown and if you weren't providing her wat, she wanted at that time of her asking then she was against you. Lanai never understood why LA 'Shay had so much hate for her. Lanai never loved LA 'Shay any less though because Lanai loved all her children regardless of their feelings towards her. Lanai always did wat was best for her children and even thought they felt like she was always working or never had money to get them everything they want, they always knew that she really tried her best to provide the best for them. Lanai was the type of person who wanted the best for her children and wanted to leave some type of legacy behind for them to have if something was to ever happen to her. Lanai is starting late on trying to own her own home but better late than never. Lanai even believes this book is going to be the key to open more doors and a better lifestyle for her and her children. Lanai had found this house in Hopkins, SC that she had fell in love with. This house was once again supposed to be a new beginning for her and Lex but since Lex does not want to help Lanai with getting the home, Lanai is going to get it on her own. Lanai was always the type of person once she asks you for help and you leave her hanging do not expect it again and that was a lot for her to even ask anyone for help. Lanai never knew how to accept help when it was just giving to her so for her to ask was a big step for her. Lanai was so determined to get this house and make it her home but only thing that was hindering her from getting the house was the down payment. Lanai father Aaron was going to send Lanai the down payment for the house, but Aaron transportation was limited in North Carolina. Lanai did not let that back-slide mess with her goal to make that house hers. Lanai was always a strong believer of things come to those who are patient and know that God is always in control. Even though she was moving away from her help she always has a plan where she will not fail to succeed in the end. Lanai just need her daughters Patient and LA 'Shay to get on board of helping her get situated once she gets the house and find a sitter for the boys while she works. Lanai is only taking the boys with her when she moves to her new home in Hopkins. Even though Lanai does not know if she is going to get approve for the property, but she kept a positive mindset to claim it into existence. Lanai does not have the best of credit because all her wrong choices she made in life; Lanai did not have anyone to teach her the importance of having a clear credit. Lanai started at a young age getting credit cards and putting things in her name for other people and ended up messing up her credit. Lanai is at a place in her life where she is trying to correct the problem to get where she wants to go. Lanai still struggling financially but it is not going to stop her from getting her dream home in the end. When Lanai first started writing this book, she knew that this was going to be her golden ticket for the new beginnings. Lanai had already had visions of herself going on television talk shows, radio interviews, and even doing conventions where she inspired many women that was going through the same stuff she was going through. Lanai always had spiritual profits speak greatness over her life and many have told her things that she did not know she had the ability of doing. Lanai was always a special person who went over and beyond to make every and anyone around her feel important and loved. Lanai heart was filled with so much love and sometimes it was a gift and a curse, but honestly, she got that from her amazing grandmother who she loved so dearly. Lanai goal is to make her grandmother Pearl so proud of her before she leaves this world. Lanai wants to have the biggest wedding and marry the love of her life and the one person she wants to be front and center is her biggest fan Grandma Pearl. Lanai would be so devastated if she don't get married before her grandmother pass away because no matter how many wrong turns Lanai has taken in her life, Grandma Pearl never judged her and was the heart of the family. Will Lanai complete her goal in getting her house and getting married before her grandmother is called home. Guess you guys will have to wait and see in the next book that is to come. Lanai has been through many trials and tribulations but that never stop her from achieving all her many accomplishments. Lanai is a strong individual who did not take nothing from anyone regardless of who they were and that came as she got older. If this book interested, you just wat for more to come. If anyone wants to speak or get any advice from Lanai personally please do not hesitate to reach out to her on her social media pages or email that will be listed below. This is how her bookings for guest appearances or speaking at any event will be conducted. Lanai is always available and open to helping anyone or giving advice. Thanks in advance for reading my book and much luv!!

Poems

Passionate Love

The way u kiss someone, the way they feel in ur
arms, the way they make u feel inside is undeniable
love.

The way they say they love u, as they look in ur
eyes, the way they passionately wipe the tears from
ur cries.

Falling in love can happen at the blank of an eye,
staying in love is to grow as one as time goes by.

Do not let temptation seduce u to fall off track, two
mins of sensation is not worth that.

Women say they want a real man in their lives, sus
stop being dumb and accept less and their lies.

Men say a real woman is hard to find but in all reality she cud be right in front of u and not even a dime.

U look for the wrong things when u want to be complete, it's not the way the person looks or how they dress that should attract u it's about the bigger picture, someone who will ride or die for u. Let this open ur eyes to opening a better future path, nothing that is temporary something that will last.

~Peace~

~Wisdom Love~

I am Me

I am me, simply beautiful, determined, self sufficient, a phenomenal black woman, who many have taken advantage of.

I smile with life like no other, my eyes glow like there is no tomorrow. Many people see how pure my heart can be and how much of a go getter I am.

No ones perfect and everyone deserves true love. See the path that I pave with greatness from behind, because u did not see me for who I am only for wat I can do.

I will succeed at all that I set my mind to do best believe my God has cleansed my pain for something new. You had me once and did not cherish this flower full of treasures. Now I am blossoming like no other.

My past is not my future, life is to short for anything less. Stay focus because greatness comes from those who are truly blessed by the grace of God. Sleep on ya girl if u want, speaking it in existence is all I know.

~As Real As It Gets~

~Wisdom Love~

Sex Drive

It can be the wettest dream,

Boy make me scream,

Come and whip this cherry til you make it cream.

Kiss me from my neck down to my G-spot,

Damn I feel so good baby, please do not stop,

You got this pussy throbbing and so take me to ur bed.

You say you are hungry, so it is dinner right between my legs,

If I squirt a little bit can you stand the rain,

I like a little pleasure mixed with a little pain.

Sitting in my bedroom thinking bout u,

Visions in my head of all the things I want to do,

I want you so bad I am feeling like an addict,

You are my addiction, u are my worse habit.

My sex drive is so high

It is shifting into overdrive,

This feeling I cannot deny

Because of my sex drive.

Spoken Truths

Tears cried over and over again

But these tears have come to an end,

U thought u hurt me and broke my heart

But as pure as I am, my heart u cannot tear apart.

Your true colors were shown to me in the darkness of the night, but God almighty shows truthfulness in the light, Your life as u know it will never be the same, Messing with a child of God I will always be ahead of the game.

U may think you have won this battle

But the best is yet to come,

While I have moved on with smiles on my own

Your heart will always and forever be numb.

I am the one and only there is none like me

Your love u think u will have for the next will bring

u pain and misery.

God have amazing plans for my life

I will be some lucky girl amazing wife,

This is just the beginning of life's journey for me

There is more to come just wait and see.

Blessings and Happiness comes to those who waits

But people who hurt others will come from the

devil hells gate!!!!

~Wisdom Love~

Sex with Me

Sex with me a fantasy of many

The sensation of my climax is as sweet as candy,

Many have tried and failed to make me squirt

My pussy so tight I made u nut first.

Sex with me makes ur dreams come true

Open my pandora box, and ur life will be open to
something new.

Just do not waist my time or I will tell u to use a toy

I love to squeeze ur dick with my clit so I can make
u cum,

Sex with me is top notch #1

Play the game right and u will be satisfied

U will remember me for the rest of ur lifetime.

~Wisdom Love~

<u>Love Dynasty</u>

Love is a word many uses in vain

Cannot help who u love it is even harder to explain,

Love is like a drug that will drive u insane

Blame only urself is the name of the game.

Stay focus of the journey that is in front of u

Your heart will open again to someone new,

Do not go looking for love let it find u

Easier said than done lord that is the truth.

I have been down this road may time before

Endless open and closed doors,

You live and learn from ur mistakes.

Best believe u can always be replaced

Like I said before I am the one and only,

And there is none like me and never will be

Watch wat I say, you will see.

~Wisdom Love~

Climax

One, Two, Three, Four

Are how many strokes to my uterus door,

As ur dick grinds in my clit so closely

Ur lips caress my breast very slowly.

As u reach my G-spot and I am about to cum

My legs began to shake and become very numb,

Now it is my turn u had ur fun.

Let the games begin u cannot run,

I climbed on top to ride ur dick.

It slides in slowly from my juicy clit,

As u know this is about to come to an end.

It does not take me long to bring it in with a win,

My pussy is a true legacy,

Test my word and fulfill ur fantasy.

U will never know til u try and see,

My word is my bond u better ask about me.

There are few who came back for more,

They will never get pass Pandora's door.

I have worked them; I am very addictive, and u will come back again.

Sorry ur time has run out and this is the end.

~Wisdom Love~

Love Untouched

Love untouched will never be broken

Love untouched is left unspoken,

Love untouched is pure as gold

Love untouched is a real I am told.

Love untouched is hard to find

Love untouched will come to u in time,

Love untouched is just a breath away

Love untouched is in your heart to stay.

~Wisdom Love~

Broken Spirits

Life full of broken spirits

By lies, hate, & deceit,

Wondering why this place we call world cannot be

filled with love, happiness, & peace.

Our people are becoming victimized because of

their race also known as “Black”,

They cannot walk the streets without being

criticized or blamed for crimes they never

committed.

Broken spirits were created from our ancestors

Who lived the life of slavery?

People like Harriet Tubman & Dr. Martin Luther King Jr. made a way for our people to have bravery to stand our ground.

Broken spirits are not just for the person who are suffering, but for those who are recovering from what they don't understand because they were never taught any different and never had the knowledge to know right from wrong.

We as people should grow and manifest as one and share our knowledge with the ones who will have to live in this democracy once we leave this world and not let this world destroy what we leave behind called our legacy.

~Peace~

~Wisdom Love~

Email: lanaijackson8482@gmail.com

FaceBook: Shaniqua Jackson

Istagram: Caramel8488

Snap:Caramel8488

BigoLive: Caramel8488 or Bo$$TastyLuv

Youtube: Shaniqua Roberts

Made in the USA
Middletown, DE
30 June 2024

56546685R00093